# Zak's King Arthur Adventure

By Adam and Charlotte Guillain

Illustrated by Charlie Alder

W

FRANKLIN WATTS

LONDON•SYDNEY

# Chapter 1

Zak had saved up for a whole year
to buy his latest gadget.

"This metal detector is going to make
me rich!" he told everyone, including
his dog, Skip.

"Woof!" said Skip.

Zak thought that he would make his
money back quickly, but after one week
all he had was –

one five pence piece,

three cans

and a dented bucket.

"I will find something that makes me rich, you'll see," Zak told Skip.

But Skip was too busy sniffing trees.

The next week, Zak and his family went on holiday to a caravan site. As soon as his parents had parked, Zak was off with his metal detector and spade. Skip ran after him, barking with excitement.

"Use the route finder on your phone,"
Mum called after him. "Don't get lost."

Zak decided to follow a path through
a nearby wood.

They ended up in a field by a large mound. "This looks like a good spot, Skip," said Zak, switching his metal detector on. After a few minutes he got a very strong signal.

"This is it, Skip!" said Zak, and he quickly started to dig. Then Zak's spade hit something hard. He reached down to find out what it was.

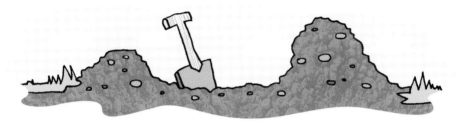

"A sword handle!" he gasped.
"I'm going to be rich!"

# Chapter 2

Zak marked his location on his phone
and raced back to the caravan site.
"Look at this!" he cried, clutching
the sword handle.

"Great," said Dad, not really looking.
"Now come in for some lunch."

"But what if it's something expensive
or really important?" Zak protested.

"Hmm," said Mum impatiently.
"Maybe you've discovered Camelot, well
done. Now go and wash your hands."

"Camelot?" Zak thought.
"That's where King Arthur lived."

Later that afternoon, Zak was sitting outside the caravan, cleaning his latest find, when an old man passed by.

"That's King Arthur's!" exclaimed the man, pointing at the sword handle.

Then the old man smiled.

"Would you like to be rich, boy?"

"Yes!" said Zak.

"Then go back to the

place where you found

that sword and look for

a hazel tree by a mound."

"Okay," said Zak.

"There you must dig into the mound."
The old man looked very serious.
"But be warned. You must only take as
much gold as you need and whatever
you do, don't ring the King's bell!"

Zak tucked the sword handle into his belt,
grabbed his phone and spade and raced off
with Skip leading the way.

# Chapter 3

It was Skip who found the hazel tree.

"Good boy," Zak panted, patting Skip's head. Zak furiously started to dig. He'd almost given up when – CLUNK!

"What was that?" Zak said.

He quickly brushed away the soil.

"Wow!" he gasped, as a stone door
opened right before his eyes.

He checked that no one was
watching and then crawled in.

After a few twists and turns, Zak started
to follow a glowing, yellow light.

Then, turning into a new tunnel,

Zak caught sight of a shadow ahead.

"What is that?"

he wondered.

To his amazement, Zak realised that it was a large bell hanging from the roof of the tunnel. He suddenly remembered the old man's warning.

"Shhh!" he told Skip. "We mustn't ring it."

He flattened his back against the wall and carefully squeezed his way around the bell while Skip crawled underneath.

"Unbelievable!" Zak exclaimed, as he found himself in a huge circular room, lit by many candles. Around the room lay a hundred sleeping knights in glistening armour, their white horses sleeping at their feet.

It was then that Zak saw a king lying on a bed, surrounded by piles of gold. "That must be King Arthur!" Zak gasped in wonder.

Zak tiptoed to the King's bed and started
to fill his pockets with gold.

"Now, take only as much gold as you
need," the old man had said.

"And I need
lots!" Zak
muttered.

He tucked his T-shirt into his jeans and
stuffed down as many coins as he could.
Then he made his way back to the tunnel.
But as he tried to squeeze past the bell,
his bulging T-shirt knocked it!

The bell started to swing and
there was an almighty chime.

"Oh no!" Zak gasped.

The knights began to stir.

"Come on Skip, run!"

But it was too late.

# Chapter 4

One of the knights grabbed Zak's feet
and dangled him upside down, shaking
him hard. Zak wiggled and kicked with
all his might.

Skip barked, snapping at the knight's heels.

As Skip bit into the knight's leg, Zak crashed to the ground. Quickly pulling himself up, Zak ran after Skip.

"Stop him!"

The bellowing voice of King Arthur was filled with rage and it shook the ground.

"We're going to be buried alive!" Zak spluttered as the tunnels filled with clouds of tumbling soil and dust.

Hearing the sound of clanking metal behind him, Zak raced blindly on, following Skip's loud barks.

"At last!" Zak gasped as he saw daylight ahead. Bursting out of the secret doorway, Zak and Skip sprinted back to the caravan.

# Chapter 5

When Zak got back to the caravan site,

he found Mum and Dad sitting in camping

chairs, reading books.

"You won't believe it," Zak wheezed.

"We've found the place where

King Arthur sleeps!"

Zak dragged Mum and Dad back to the spot where he had found the sword handle. "This is just a cow field," said Dad.

"But there was a mound here and a hazel tree," Zak protested. "I found a secret tunnel that led to a special room where King Arthur was sleeping."

But, strangely, there was no sign that a mound or a hazel tree had ever been there. "Never mind," said Mum. "Come on, let's go for a swim."

"My pockets were full of gold," Zak said,

reaching into his empty pockets.

"And your head is full
of dreams,"
sighed Dad.

Zak looked at Skip.
"I wish you could talk,"
he thought.
"Woof," said Skip.

"Well, you have got the sword handle," said Mum. Zak checked his belt but even the sword handle was gone.

"I don't believe it!" he cried, throwing up his arms.

"Don't worry," said Mum, kindly.

"You still have a great story."

Zak looked at Mum, disappointed.

"But will anyone believe it?" he wondered.

First published in 2012 by
Franklin Watts
338 Euston Road
London
NW1 3BH

Franklin Watts Australia
Level 17/207 Kent Street
Sydney
NSW 2000

Text © Adam and Charlotte Guillain 2012
Illustration © Charlie Alder 2012

Series Editor: Melanie Palmer
Series Advisor: Catherine Glavina
Series Designer: Peter Scoulding

A CIP catalogue record for this book is
available from the British Library.

ISBN 978 1 4451 0778 3 (hbk)
ISBN 978 1 4451 0784 4 (pbk)

Printed in China

Franklin Watts is a division of Hachette
Children's Books, an Hachette UK company.
www.hachette.co.uk